The Crocodile's Christmas Jandals

by Margaret Mahy

pictures by Deirdre Gardiner

READY TO READ

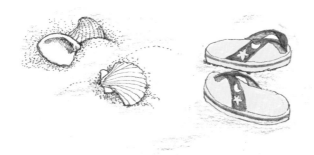

LEARNING MEDIA
WELLINGTON

The crocodile loved his Christmas jandals.
His Aunt Alligator
had given them to him.
They were blue jandals
with golden stars and silver moons.
When the crocodile wore them,
he felt his feet
were always walking in party time.

4

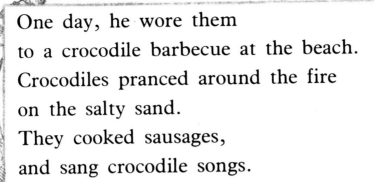

One day, he wore them
to a crocodile barbecue at the beach.
Crocodiles pranced around the fire
on the salty sand.
They cooked sausages,
and sang crocodile songs.

> "Sing a song of merry crocs
> Taking off their shoes and socks,
> Stretching out their merry claws,
> Drinking lemonade through straws."

The crocodile took off his Christmas jandals
and put them side by side on the beach.
He pranced and sang and cooked sausages
with the other crocodiles
until the barbecue was over.
Then he went to get his jandals.
Horrakapotchkin!

The tide had come in
while he was prancing and singing.
It had stolen
his left foot Christmas jandal.

The crocodile ran up and down the beach,
but he couldn't find it.
His left foot Christmas jandal
had floated out to sea.

Just as he was going home,
dragging his tail sadly,
the crocodile saw another jandal—
a left foot red rubber one—
lying among the shells.

"You've brought me the wrong one!"
said the crocodile crossly
to the waves.
The waves just rustled on the sand,
and said nothing.

The next Friday,
there were football matches at school.
The Crocodiles were going to play
the Girls and Boys.

The crocodile went along to cheer
for the Crocodiles.
He had to wear his odd jandals—
a right foot Christmas jandal
and a left foot red rubber jandal.
"Hooray!" he shouted.
"Hooray! Come on the Crocodiles!"

The girl next to him was cheering
for the Girls and Boys.

"Hooray!" she shouted.
"Hooray! Hooray!"
She shouted very loudly
and stamped her feet.

The crocodile looked at her feet.
She was wearing
a right foot red rubber jandal.
On her left foot she was wearing
a beautiful blue jandal
with golden stars and silver moons!

"You've got my Christmas jandal!"
shouted the crocodile.

The girl looked at the crocodile's feet.
"And you've got my red rubber holiday jandal!"
she cried.

"I found it on the beach near my house,"
the crocodile said.
"I was looking for mine,
and I found yours instead."

"I found *yours* on the beach near *my* house,"
said the girl.
"I was looking for mine,
and I found yours instead."

"The sea stole them
and swapped them over,"
said the crocodile.

The girl and the crocodile
wore odd jandals all day,
and watched football together.

The crocodile cheered for the Crocodiles,
but sometimes he cheered for the Girls and Boys—
just for a change.

The girl cheered for the Girls and Boys,
but sometimes she cheered for the Crocodiles—
just for a change.

At the end of the day,
the girl gave the crocodile
his left foot Christmas jandal.
The crocodile gave the girl
her left foot red rubber jandal.

"See you next football day!"
the crocodile called.
"We'll swap jandals again, shall we?
Just for fun!"

Then he pranced home.
His feet glittered with golden stars
and silver moons.
He was walking with both feet
in party time once more.

You will meet the crocodile again in

The Bubbling Crocodile
Shopping with a Crocodile
A Crocodile in the Garden
A Crocodile in the Library